PAT CUMMINGS

CAROUSEL

BRADBURY PRESS NEW YORK

Maxwell Macmillan Canada Toronto
Maxwell Macmillan International
New York Oxford Singapore Sydney

LIBRARY OF CONGRESS CATALOGING-IN-PUBLICATION DATA
Cummings, Pat.
Carousel / written and illustrated by Pat Cummings.—1st ed.
p.   cm.
Summary: Alex's father misses her birthday party, and everything
is spoiled until the animals on his gift of a tiny carousel come to life.
ISBN 0-02-725512-3
[1. Birthdays—Fiction.   2. Fathers and daughters—Fiction.
3. Merry-go-round—Fiction.   4. Animals—Fiction.]   I. Title.
PZ7.C9148Car   1994
[E]—dc20   93-8708

For Gloria Mintz Smith
and the Tiffany Place Gang

Alex didn't want her hair braided or her shiny shoes buckled or every single little pearly button buttoned on her dress. And she definitely didn't want her birthday cake after dinner with just her aunts.

"Where's Daddy?" she grumbled for the eighth time.

"Hold still, Alex," sighed her mother, tugging away.

Off went the sneakers. On went the bows. Off went the jeans. On came the frills.

Dinner lasted forever. Alex pushed peas from side
to side on her plate. She stabbed a potato chunk with
her fork, dragged it through the gravy, and ate it like an
ice-cream cone.

"Alex," her mother warned, and then smiled at the
aunts. "Let's open your presents before we cut the cake."

Before Alex could say, "Let's wait for Daddy," her
aunts had whisked away the dinner dishes, pulled
balloons out of bags, and popped party hats on every-
one's heads. There was a pile of presents to open.

Alex opened Auntie Lea's gift first. "I have a *million* pairs of pajamas," she mumbled grumpily.

She unwrapped a frothy ballerina tutu from Aunt Ruby. Aunt Ruby liked things to sparkle. "Looks scratchy," Alex fussed under her breath. Her mother made a face at her, but Alex didn't care.

Then, burrowing through puffs of tissues, Alex found a pair of long, fuzzy, hot pink slipper-socks. They had rabbit ears and googly eyes and WHISKERS! Aunt Rose scurried to grab her camera.

"No way," Alex groaned.

"Alex!" her mother said sharply. "Maybe you need to go to bed." Alex quickly hugged her aunts and thanked them. She wasn't mad at *them*. "But Daddy promised . . ." she began.

"He said he'd try, honey. And," her mother added, handing
her the last gift, "he said to give you this just in case he didn't
get back from his trip in time." Alex felt her cheeks
getting hot. *He knew he wouldn't be home!* She
tugged at the paper and yanked off the ribbons.
"Ooooooooohhh . . . aaaaaahhhh!"
the aunts cried. There before her was
the most perfect little carousel that
Alex had ever seen.

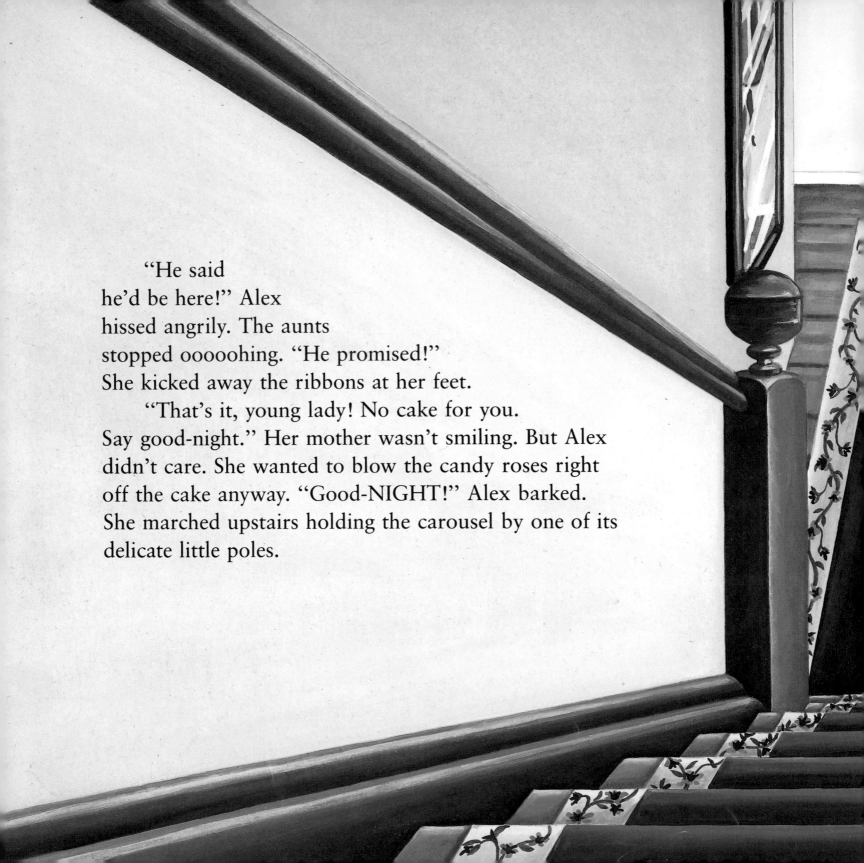

"He said
he'd be here!" Alex
hissed angrily. The aunts
stopped ooooohing. "He promised!"
She kicked away the ribbons at her feet.
    "That's it, young lady! No cake for you.
Say good-night." Her mother wasn't smiling. But Alex
didn't care. She wanted to blow the candy roses right
off the cake anyway. "Good-NIGHT!" Alex barked.
She marched upstairs holding the carousel by one of its
delicate little poles.

"I don't care." Alex twisted the bows out of her hair and pulled off her party dress without stopping to undo a single little button. "He knew it. He knew it," she fussed at the little animals.

Alex heard her aunts laughing downstairs. "They're eating up my cake!"

She jumped into bed, kicked the blankets back, and sent the carousel tumbling. There was a soft snap. Slowly, she picked up the carousel and studied it. The tiny zebra looked wobbly. With just a wiggle, it broke off completely!

Its little painted face looked almost angry. She had to fix the carousel before her father came home, or he would think she didn't like her gift. She yawned. She turned. There would be time in the morning. . . .

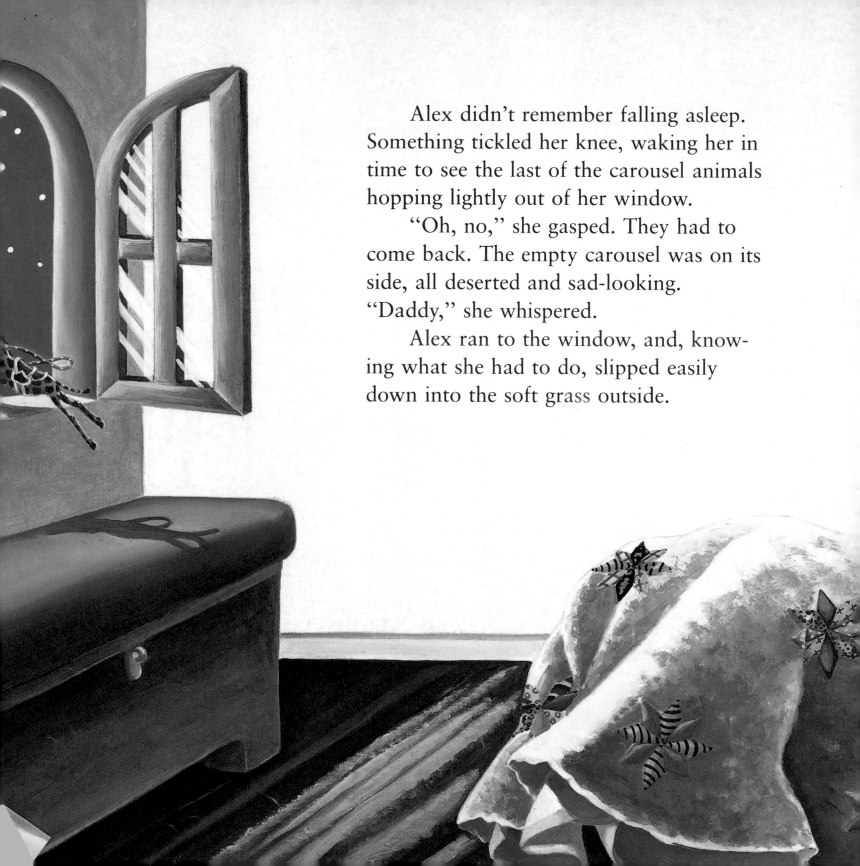

Alex didn't remember falling asleep. Something tickled her knee, waking her in time to see the last of the carousel animals hopping lightly out of her window.

"Oh, no," she gasped. They had to come back. The empty carousel was on its side, all deserted and sad-looking. "Daddy," she whispered.

Alex ran to the window, and, knowing what she had to do, slipped easily down into the soft grass outside.

The animals were getting away!
Alex took off running. Even as she
hurried after them, it seemed
that the moonlight was
making them grow, their
legs stretching farther
and farther. A paw here,
ears there, whiskers
in and out of the blue
nighttime leaves.

And just when she thought
she had lost them forever, Alex saw
them waiting beyond the tall trees.
They were waiting for her.
Alex tiptoed up to the zebra. She carefully
climbed up on his back. A little bit of
pole was sticking up just where she
had broken it off. "Sorry,"
she whispered in his ear.
Had he heard her?

The zebra
shook his mane
and began to trot. Then he galloped,
then he flew. Around and around and
around, all of the animals were running
with him. From frog to flamingo,
from rabbit to giraffe, Alex took
turns: upside down, right side
up, one hand, no hands,
both eyes closed.

When at last they slowed
down, Alex found she was again
on the zebra's back. One by one, the
sleepy animals made their way through the
cool grass toward her bedroom window.
Alex curled her fingers in and out of
the zebra's mane. Even in the
pale light, she could see that
he was smiling.

One eye opened. Then the other. It was morning.

"Oh, dear!" Alex sat straight up. She remembered everything. She remembered the carousel animals had all gotten loose. She pulled the covers apart, but now there wasn't a single little animal in sight. She rolled onto the floor and peered under the bed. No flamingo. No leopard. Nothing!

"Happy birthday, sleepyhead. You awake?" Her father was home! Hugging Alex, he kissed her smack on the nose. Then he saw the carousel sitting underneath the window.

"Daddy, I'm sorry I broke it," Alex said.

"And I'm sorry I missed your birthday," her father answered. "I got really angry when my plane was so late in coming home. But I couldn't stay angry. Know why?"

Alex shook her head.

"Because the same thing that made me angry made me happy when I thought about it. I was happy just to be coming home."

"Breakfast, anyone?" her mother asked, going straight to the window to close it. "It got a bit windy in here last night." She winked at Alex.

Alex kissed them both.

"We have a little work to do," her dad said, pressing the tiny zebra into Alex's hand. "What's for breakfast?"

"Oh, scrambled cake and ice-cream omelettes." Her mother laughed and headed downstairs.

Alex took her dad by the hand.

"And put on those cute little slippers for Daddy, Alex!" her mother called out.

Alex squeezed her dad's hand. He was going to *love* those slippers!